INDIGENOUS, I AM

Niłtooli Wilkins

Illustrations by Berglind Bjornsdottir

INDIGENOUS, I AM

Copyright © 2021 Niłtooli Wilkins

All rights reserved.

ISBN: 979-8725449600

DEDICATION

This collection is for any young or old soul that feels as if their voice goes unnoticed or does not matter. It does, it always has, and you will find it again.

INDIGENOUS, I AM

ACKNOWLEDGMENTS

I'd like to thank all of my friends who took the time to read my words and provide honest feedback and love while I was writing. I'd like to thank my family for their constant support and encouragement. A special shout-out to Shimá for her guidance and unwavering love through every phase of my life. I remember being little reading her poetry and being inspired at such a young age by her words.

Thank you to my incredibly supportive partner, who walked beside me every step of the way through this process, and who believed in me when I didn't believe in myself.

Lastly, thank you to the Creator for listening to my doubts, fears, and my prayers.

INDIGENOUS, I AM

Contents

Growing 5
    The Night My Voice Was Taken 6
    Squeeze My Heart 8
    Brown-Eyed Native Girl 10
    Naked 13
    Interwoven 16
    His Chair 18
    The Wall 20

Trauma 23
    Intergenerational Trauma 24
    Unhinged 26
    My Body Is Mine 28

Becoming 31
    My Mother's Eyes 32
    The Creator Gave Me 34
    Letter to a Flower 36
    It's Okay 38
    Connection 40
    Ancestors' Blood 41
    Pipe Ceremony 42
    Harmony 44
    Honey 46
    It Wasn't Your Fault 48
    Dressed in Turquoise 50
    Energies 52
    Fighting women 54

The Night She Found Me 57

Horizon 60

Ballads of my path 62

About The Author 65

More From Eaglespeaker Publishing 67

Growing

The Night My Voice Was Taken
(TW: sexual trauma)

I was so young, seeped in adolescence
It happened within the four walls of a childhood home I'll never forget
My parents and brothers were in other rooms, oblivious to any danger
Safely under one roof

Silent, mute, speechless

I knew them, so this must be ok
They held my innocent trust in their palms like a fragile infant
Cradled it, made sure not to startle it awake
They know me, so what they are doing must be acceptable

My insides unnerved
My skin crawled as they took their turns
I am at a loss as to what is transpiring
around me and inside me

That's when my voice left my body
My words were so far away, so out of reach

Silent, mute, speechless

These snapshot images and scenes flickered
in my mind throughout my young adulthood
I was unable to place them, connect with them, recognize them
Were they even my experiences to carry?

Surely all children have had this experience
Did this all happen or was this one of my reoccurring nightmares?

"That was sexual trauma."
Words said with empathy from my first therapist

Silent, mute, speechless yet again

My childlike brain had done its part after it happened
It protected me as a mother bear protects her cubs
By storing those memories away in a locked chest
and shoving it into the depths of the sea

Once I found that chest a different version of me rose to surface
Anger, irritation, why me?
I threw the blame onto myself and I felt it like a
weighted blanket wrapped around my shoulders

I was there, I could have stopped it
Why didn't I say no?
Why didn't I trust *myself* and not **them?**
Why was my voice useless to me then?

Rage, confusion, betrayal

All these new emotions swirled above, around and through me
It was all exiting me slowly, slowly, slowly
releasing what was caged up in a separate area of myself
My voice had found me again

Years and years of looking for each other
Years and years of silence, rendering speechless
Screams and aches on the inside trying to knife
their way through my layers

I open my mouth long and wide as a snake
before it devours its prey
And I scream and scream and scream
Into a pillow, out of my car window, at myself, at them
But nonetheless, I can scream

I don't know silence like I once did

Squeeze My Heart

Squeeze my tender heart
and steal the air in my lungs
Take me away from this moment
of heat-filled eyes, and penetrating questions

I am no longer here
Sensations left my side
Sight, taste, touch
I am frozen, immobile

My emotions surround me
each one poking me, prodding me
to release
My taste arrives

I taste the saltiness of my tears
as they trickle down to my quivering lips
I see my reflection and I am here
I am shaking, my body is speaking to me

Squeeze my heart
fill my lungs with air

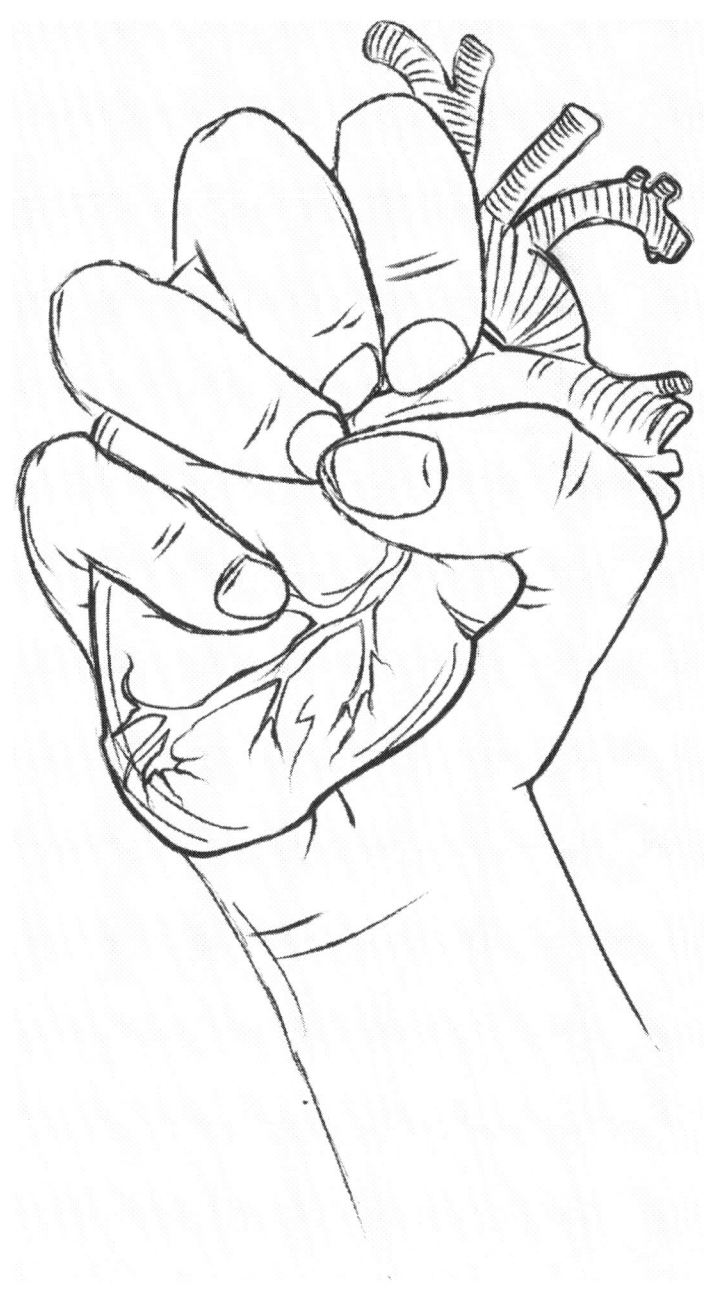

Brown-Eyed Native Girl

Brown-eyed native girl.
Avoids seeing her reflection,
she doesn't love what stares back.
She sees dirtiness splashed across the mirror
paired with what was behind it.

Dirt, dirt, dirty.

In her circle she only saw sea foam speckled eyes,
piercing blue and round as nickels,
that only glistened brighter in the sunlight.
Blue was desirable, as a cloudless sky.
Sought after and magical to her.
Brown was muddy filled with dullness.

Dirt, dirt, dirty.

She didn't understand why her eyes matched the land and
that it was a reminder of where she came from,
and those before her.
She didn't know that her eyes also sparkled during golden hour,
as she often closed them,
blinding her from the many
shades of chocolate sprinkled with lighter beams.
She wasn't aware that her eyes represented the roots below her,

spider-like spread out in the ground.
A foundation for growth that is everchanging.

Dirt, dirt, dirty like soil.

Soil is the birthplace and home of
the ground we walk upon.
She didn't know she carried all of this power
and wisdom with her.

She only thought she was a
brown-eyed native girl.

INDIGENOUS, I AM

Naked

How do I love the parts of me that
I don't even like the sight of?
What I see in my mist-filled bathroom mirror
may differ from what others see.

Bushy, brown, hair.

Frantically trying to tame the light brown baby hairs
shaping my oval full face.
Tie it up, pull it back, clip it all away.
Hide all of my length, waterfall waves, and how it beams
brighter under the sun.

Muscular, rolls, curvy.

"You've gotten chubby little one."
I try to swallow this with a pressed smile while inside it feels
as if a quarter horse kicked me in my gut.
What cutting words spoken to such innocence.
Each word an individual dagger slicing me raw.

Stripped, judgement, invisible.

How do I love these parts of me?

The parts of me that were part of my ancestors.

Wide noses, round backside, hair as thick as molasses.

Clothes weren't made with curvaceous little Native girls in mind.

How do I love these parts that they've touched?

I feel nude when I'm fully clothed.

The heat of others' eyes scorching my skin's surface.

I can't hide my body anymore.

Do they see the handprints seared on to my skin?

Do they see how dirty I feel?

All the parts of me I keep behind closed curtains.

Myself versus everyone.

And I feel so,

naked naked naked

INDIGENOUS, I AM

Interwoven

Mind, body, spirit.
Their strength and pride hanging
in three strands past their backsides.

My younger brother's hair was thin and
honeyed at the ends.
His baby hairs a lighter shade,
resembling the delicate tips of a
paint brush's bristles.

The length streamed down and in between
my adolescent fingers as I brushed out the
many tangles of being a child.
Merging hair pieces together
creating a rhythm.

Interwoven.
The mind, body and spirit.

My older brother's hair was full of thickness.
One could grab handfuls of it,
but there would still be more.
Heavy and dense as a horse's tail.

Others mocking voices of ignorance echoed.

They saw boys wafting in femininity.
I saw our culture draped amongst their shoulders.

They didn't comprehend what I
admired as their power and force.
I saw their length,
and their braids gave me conviction.

Interweaving us in
mind, body and spirit.

His Chair

I found him sitting in the dark.
Crouched in his favorite chair in the corner,
his hand covered his mouth in attempt
to muffle his bellowing sobs.

My heart cried and slashed inside me.
My curious eyes had never seen my dad
surrounded in such pain and defeat.

I knew him as himself, my father.
Goofy, proper, thoughtful.
Leaving notes of love on my pillow.

Loving words written
by someone that only knew formality.
Loss and grief greeted him while he slept.
Stealing intricate parts of him in the dusk.

Others thought of him as a God,
dressed in intellect and charisma.
Calm, composed, and charming
were the masks he wore.

But I saw that man draped in the black of night.
I saw the first man I ever loved,
and all of his agony and sorrows drenching him.

Days passed. I sat.
Years passed. I sat.
I sat in his chair in the corner,
and tried to feel what he felt.

INDIGENOUS, I AM

Embody it, be it.
Sit where he sat, in his familiar darkness,
encircled by the howls and screeches of his aching past.

Searching for the stolen parts of him,
to uncover what he kept hidden,
to see what my father looked like
from the inside.
To feel the weight that his
favorite chair felt.

The Wall

My mother's hair was a thousand
shades of the sky at midnight.
Silky smooth just as a raven's
wings after a storm.

She was a cocktail of an angered and loving woman.
She hid all her boiling emotions inside until they cascaded over
leaving remnants of internal cuts and burns.
"Speak daughter, speak to me."

Our relationship was cloaked in fragility and sameness.
I was a part of her, her warm nest my shelter and safety.
She gave and gave and gave,
often leaving herself forgotten.

"What do you feel inside daughter?"
I felt nothing & everything all bundled up inside.
As my mouth opened, the words in my head spinning and multiplying,
nothing ever came out to her.

The wall between us was invisible yet impenetrable.
Her wisdom seeped through small crevices,
entering my soul like beams of light rays.
I'd see glimpses of myself in her.
In her rage, her nurturance, her fear.

Each year we would chisel away pieces of the invisible wall.
But its height seemed unreachable.
"Speak up daughter, speak up."
A hard fist to my gut each time I'd hear her pleas.

My words were soaked in doubt.
Doubt of myself,
doubt of my truth,
doubt of my mother.

Would she believe me?
Or would the barrier between us
inevitably reach the midnight sky
we prayed to.

INDIGENOUS, I AM

Trauma

Intergenerational Trauma

I fucking hate being a statistic.
The cycle perpetuated by
unawareness enveloped in fear.

My mother was abused, and her mother and her mother before her.
This entity lives and travels from body to body
being passed on through generations.

This ball of energy goes unseen by
the outside but underneath our chest, behind our eyes,
and in our blood stream it is creating havoc unbeknownst to all.

The women before me witnessed horrific scenes.
I carry those with me wherever I go.
They live on and steal the breaths I take.

They blur my vision making my path slippery and unsteady.
All of my self-doubt or internalized thought patterns came with me
as I entered the world thirty years ago.

I fucking hate being a statistic.
This cycle of continuous merry-go-round pain,
circular and up and down we ride.

This entity that has created a home inside me has served its time.
I will write you out of me, sing you away,
stomp my feet into the earth and dance away from you,
ending you with poetry slowly grasping the life out of you.

Unhinged

Mind is up in flames, firing non-stop.
The imagery so powerful it feels like reality.
Chest is tight and unyielding.

I can feel the heat generate and spread
outward and through my entire body.
Palms collect sweat as easily as leaves collect droplets of rain.

I'm no longer here.

I'm living both feet in the past.
Tears pierce the backs of my eyelids,
unable to catch or prevent their inevitable escape.

My jaw relentlessly clenches,
the tension continues to unfurl down to my shoulders.
My hands grasping nothing but nothingness.

My lower body devoid of all feeling, movement, awareness.
A monumental wave of all senses *muted* washes over,
under and above me,
trying its hardest to knock me down but I sit motionless.

Heart has a mind of its own and is singing and dancing so loudly.
It wants to be heard. I'm sitting in this.
This deafening silence.

My blood is boiling over, and the little girl in me is howling.

Look at me.
Notice me.
Hear me.
Validate me.
Listen to me.
Believe me.

And above all,
protect me and wrap me in
something or someplace **safe.**

These thoughts bounce in and out of my mind regularly,
needing them from others but ***needing*** them from myself more.
Once the air travels back to my lungs and my chest loosens, I unclench
my fists.

I hold my beating, so very *alive* heart
like I would a delicate newborn.
My tears have dried but invited themselves back.

I greet my senses. I'm here again. I am present.
I whisper the words all parts of me need to hear.
Do I believe them? No.

Will I ever?
My wounded fearful self and the gremlins
inside me laugh and say, "no."

The innocent, loving, cherished
child inside me simply
smiles and says, "Yes."

My Body Is Mine

Golden-kissed skin in the summer.
White lines shaped as a singlet are
remnants of the suns force.
It is mine.

The valley of my back, and the hills of my backside.
The arches of my shoulders, bent knees, and arms.
Learning to love every bend and every area that creates movement
is constantly evolving.

There are rolls of my stomach I can cling to in times of self-pity.
It is mine. Mine to love.
Mine to touch.
Mine to truly see.

It has voyaged through turbulent times,
sometimes at the hands of myself.
Often at the hands of others.
I didn't recognize it.

It didn't feel like my own.
I was separated from it, and *they* placed an ocean between us.
They tried to keep us apart because they knew if we were one,
they wouldn't have us.

INDIGENOUS, I AM

I am here now, fully.
It is mine to love.
Mine to touch.
Mine to really see.

I am still becoming one with it and
all it's oddly scenic parts.
It has scars that are visible,
and scars that are veiled.

But now we are here, melting together.
They will not separate us again.
You are mine, and you are bound in worthiness.

INDIGENOUS, I AM

Becoming

My Mother's Eyes

"Would you have stopped it from happening, mom?"
The words I'd always wished to utter
had exited my lips and
her answer soothed and embraced
the delicate child in me.

The wall seemed to diminish before us.
As I saw my mother's pain displayed
in tearful sobs,
I saw where my wisdom was born.

I saw where our pasts intertwined,
and that her blood and sorrow circled through me.
I saw our fears and trauma under a telescope.
Connecting us and giving birth
to this new bond.

I looked in my mother's dark copper eyes,
and truly saw
my own reflection.

INDIGENOUS, I AM

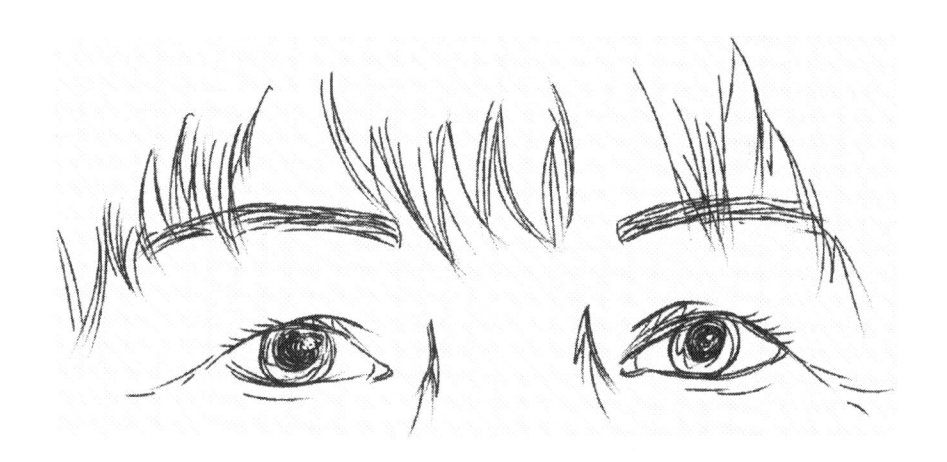

The Creator Gave Me

The Creator gave me two eyes.
To see the souls of others--to relate.

The Creator gave me a nose to take a breath
and smell the aromas of the earth.
The dancing petals of a flower and the soil that nourishes it.
The warm asphalt after a summer's rainfall,
the comfort of warm coffee on a lazy morning.
The scrumptious waft of a new baby as they exude purity.

The Creator gave me lips to part.
In a smile, an intimate encounter,
a tongue to lick off the remnants
left by the ocean's salty waters.
To savor the first sip of grandma's southern sweet tea.

The Creator gave me two hands.
To caress the edges and nooks of her face.
Two arms to get wrapped up in her.

The Creator gave me two legs
to travel through life and its peaks and unsteady paths.
The forward strides, stagnant standing and backwards steps
are all movement and gathered experiences.

The Creator gave me a heart.

Meant to repair and then expand
with every break, bruise or damage.

With my head submerged underwater
each beat is so evident and clear in its message to me.
I am alive, and I hold everything I need.

Letter to a Flower

Your petals whisper to me
As I kneel down I wonder why you
pull me towards you with every breath
Striking to look at, yes

Your bright colors radiate and hold my gaze
I ponder and realize it's because of your very nature
Your roots are grown in Mother Earth,
soiled, and given strength

You are born into your beauty, as you are and
much like human beings are
We are brought into this world as we are
raw, natural, lovely as such

As we grow up, some bend and contort their bodies to fit in a box
Some wish to be someone or something else
It's inherent, the desire to belong
But we must remember, the way of the flower

I simply can't forget, as I am drawn to you
and your divine being
Standing tall, colorful, prancing in the wind
You inspire me to be just as I am

Vibrant, striking, dancing through life
The desire to be myself speaks so loudly
alongside the hum to blend in
So I will share my beauty

I will dance in the wind
I will stand tall
I will only lower myself to sit with you,
and say thank you

INDIGENOUS, I AM

It's Okay

It's okay to feel like
you won't get better
It's okay to wonder if
these feelings will last forever

We are all on our own journeys
to our spiritual self
We all can be a little gentler with
our process and our tender selves

It's okay to have fits of rage or
punch your pillow out of anger
It's okay to feel so very deeply
like that of a dagger

If you can remember to care for
and love your inner child
You can have a closer sense of
balance and still remain wild

It's okay to have an
overwhelming fear of being happy
To lean into gratefulness and
appreciate vulnerability

We all want to be seen,
loved and to feel safe
And it's okay if inside yourself,
is where you find that grace

Connection

I have an unquenchable thirst
for connection
As deep as the roots
we walk upon

Intertwining and weaving
in the soil and depths of Mother Earth
I have no more desire to
wade in the shallow parts of a still pond

Push me further under
Submerge me and all the comfort of my logics
Let's lift each other out of
the blackness that we exist in come nightfall

I promise if you bare me your soul,
I won't see your rawness
as ugly or weak,
but as wonder and strength.

Ancestors' Blood

My ancestors' blood runs through me
Their anguish, joy, lessons
My parents' stories live and breathe in me
Their trauma, love, teachings

My skin is brown, and a darker caramel hue come summer
Golden, strong and deep like our land
My hair is dark and abundant,
like buffalo hide in the midst of a bitter winter

The Creator lives in the trees outside,
in the crashing waves, or still lakes we float on
The Creator runs through me,
as my ancestors' blood is what keeps me alive

Pipe Ceremony

Senses awakened as we sit
in this tight circle
I used to dread it
As I knew my insides would be displayed

Sage and sweetgrass burn, massaging
the body of my nostrils
I breathe in and let it
marinate all parts of me

I smell healing among us

I peak and see the souls I cherish surround me
Each body arranged in the comfort that suits them
Smiles of agreeance and gratefulness,
mournful tears walk hand in hand with those of rejoice

I see healing among us

An entity that hovers around, sits beside us,
and places its hand among our hearts
Prayers grow into a symphony of release
One footprint closer to becoming centered

I hear healing among us
In our pains,
our inquiries,
our acceptance

The sacred pipe is lit and passed to each person
I fill my mouth with tobacco while it interlaces with saliva
My taste buds moan creating
a taste of home and safety before it travels to my lungs

I taste healing among us

INDIGENOUS, I AM

As the smoke leaves my parted lips, my current pain escapes
My breathing, as rhythmic as footsteps on an evening stroll
Peace has been restored,
if only for this current moment together

Arms embracing shoulders, fingers brushing away tears
like that of a fallen eyelash
I feel our connection stronger than
the blood in our veins

The connection to the heartbeat of this earth and its beings
To the spirits listening to our pleas
Senses heightened,
I feel healing among us and within me

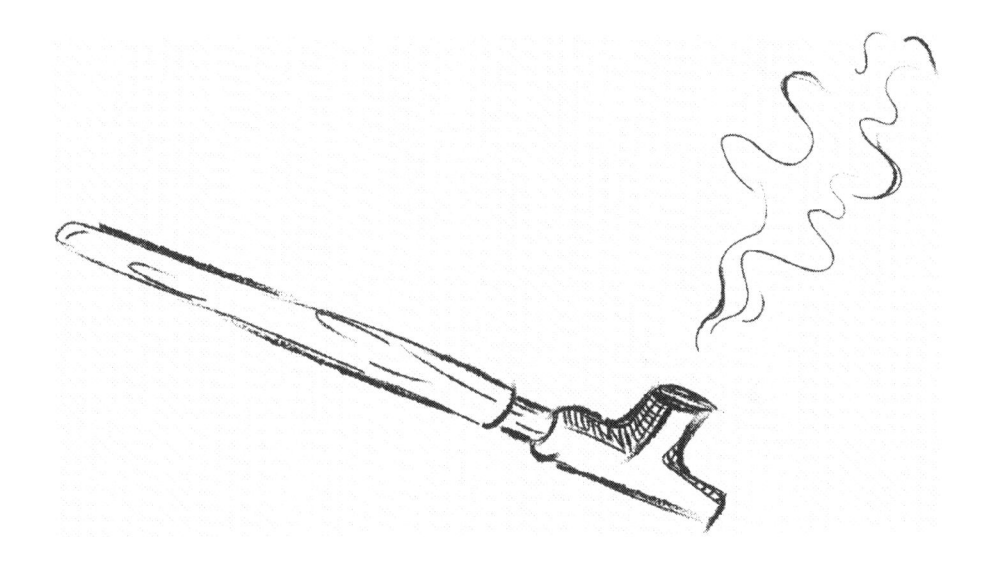

Harmony

Fear lives inside me
It's built a nest
a comfortable space to lay
in the many shades of darkness

Brightness lives inside me
It resides in all the corners of my body
Jagged beams of light poking my skins interior
Such a desire to exit my body and be noticed

It's a continuous tango for this pair
with one leading one minute
and the other taking over the next
They push and shove in desperate attempt to steal the spotlight

Soon they will learn that they can exist simultaneously
They can master the steps together
taking turns leading and being unafraid of each other
It's possible to harmoniously dance as one

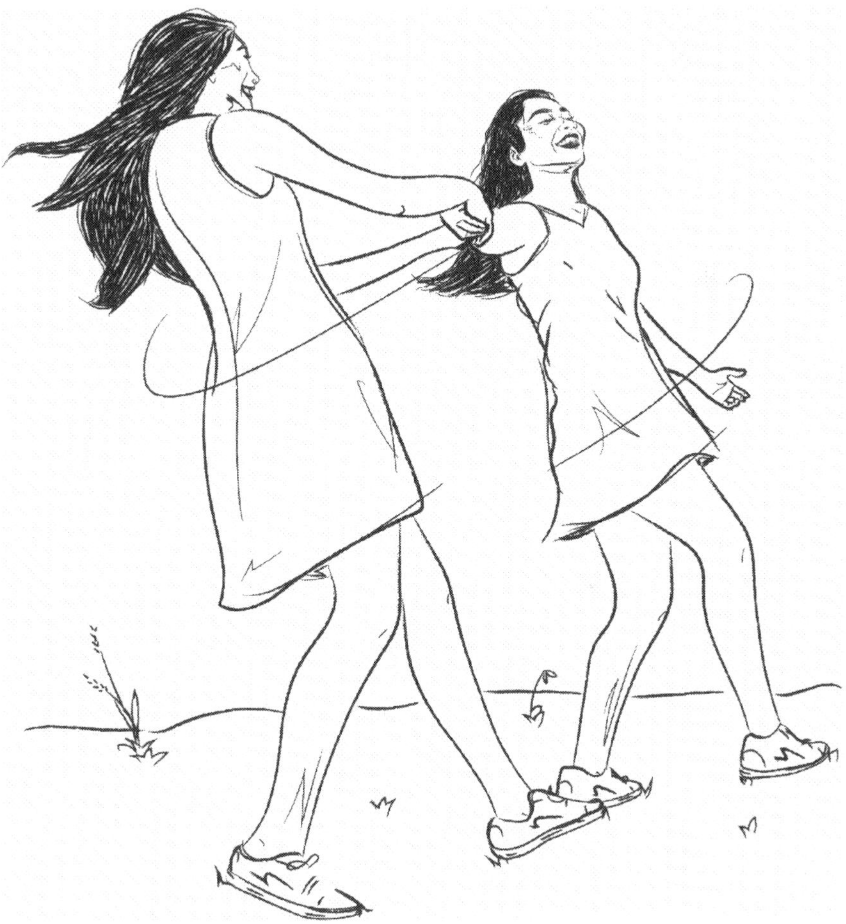

Honey

This skin is my armor
Sun rays kiss my
skin and it glows
a deeper shade

Its wounds however faded
leave fragments of my past
Its deep chestnut tone tells
stories of my ancestors

You may see dirt
I see earth that is our land
You may see my shade, and place yourself superior
I know where I came from

You may see only a brown woman
I know resilience
You may equate darkness with unworthiness
I know who I am

This shield protects me
What's underneath is a whistling heart
that's been damaged and
tenderly pieced back together

INDIGENOUS, I AM

Two lungs that clutch for air

A soul that has wandered

Been lost

Found her way

What's underneath is

no different than you

My honey-colored skin

It Wasn't Your Fault

Young one, it wasn't your fault
They held your innocence in their
palms like a fragile piece of art

Sweet soul, it wasn't your fault
I know you fight with intrusive
thoughts, as they live inside you,
cutting you from inside out

Precious one, it wasn't your fault
You blame yourself for not speaking,
not trusting your voice
It still wasn't your fault

Little one you'll see

Once a quivering flower,
your petals will grow back stronger,
rooted firmly in
resilience

INDIGENOUS, I AM

Dressed in Turquoise

She was dressed in turquoise
Dusk recognized itself in the
shadows of her hair

She did not choose her trauma
The years of fighting this nameless
pain left her exhausted and scarred

So she laid her clenched fists to rest
beside her every night
She was dressed in turquoise

It made her feel alive in her power,
and that those who walked before her
would recognize her strides

She walked with the conviction
and knowledge that she is and
will never be, alone

INDIGENOUS, I AM

Energies

I have a pair of eagles
wings inside me

one side is delicate
fragile to the touch

with feathers of nurturing
energy and softness

my femininity lives here

the other side is cloaked
in defiance

with feathers sharp to the touch and intimidating
rage and strength holding them in place

my masculinity lives here

these wings have been clipped and damaged,
with one side carrying more of the weight one day,
and the other taking over the next

they sometimes push and tug at each other
believing their way is the right way
the only way

but it is when they are taking flight in unison,
in a silent harmony where neither is right or wrong,
or better or worse

when they are balanced in how they ride each
wave of the winds

that is when they can soar infinitely, equally
in their oneness

Fighting Women

I come from a long line of
fighting women
these voices of resilient women
before me, circulate through me
and within me
I walked through life unknowingly
for too long
unknowing of their power
their force
their wisdom
their pain
their trauma
we've bled the same blood
cried the same tears
carried the same pain
when my legs have felt too heavy
to keep going
I've felt their sturdy legs and
purposeful footprints
begin to walk for me
pushing each foot in front of the other,
as they had already walked through
all that I have been fearful of
for me

INDIGENOUS, I AM

INDIGENOUS, I AM

The Night She Found Me

A wintery Saturday night
Sitting in a comfortable silence as the tv flickered
The plant medicine had entered my system
It started small, like a delicate snowflake floating around me

Questions engulfed me, my thoughts had intruded and
the mental movies had begun their reruns
The snowflake gradually built up to a snowball
that quickly descended down a steep hill

Gathering more droplets of information
Triggered, triggered, triggered
This time was unique
It was unfamiliarity meshed with terror

One minute I was here, thirty years old
And the next minute I was watching her take over my body
I was seven years old again
Rubbing my eyes, hiding my face

Hitting myself with angered fists
she had taken over, and her presence
was as powerful as an earthquake's damage
She sobbed, yelled, demanded

She was finished with sitting in four walls of deafening silence
Anger, disgust, blame
She spoke words through me that I had only written about
I knew I was not in my body

"I'm disgusting."
"Where's my mom?"
"Would she have stopped it?"
I'm not here, I'm not here, I'm not here

She didn't want to be there
She believed she held all the fault
Speak, speak, speak
I had never felt connected to her or to the
bruised and battered parts of me

I kept a strong distance because
if I believed in it,
what kind of person would I be?
Believe me, believe me, believe me

She wanted my attention after all these years of being secluded
My love, my understanding, my validation
The night greeted us as the stars painted the black canvas of the sky
She gave me my body back as my senses arose from their slumber

I never felt closer to her
She had been searching,
needing to be with me
And I needed her

She found me that night
She gifted me my voice back
And in turn I promised I'd keep her safe
And that she held none of the fault

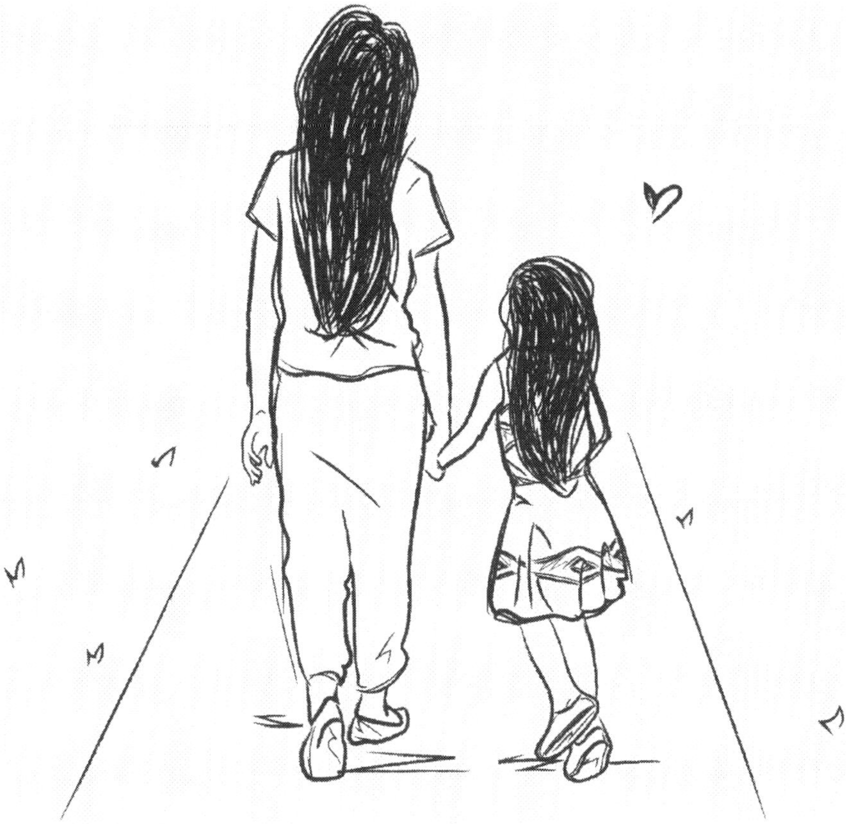

Horizon

The ball of fire crests the skyline

where the earth and the sky become one

I can see my future and it is vibrant

with colors and faces

My past lives on in me,

but I will no longer be handcuffed and confined to it

I foresee more hardships ahead

Heartbreaks to come, losses to endure

But I also see the smiling eyes of my child

A bundle of innocence to hold,

that will be a new part of me entering this world

They have already paid me a visit in my dreams, to check if it's their time to come

The horizon was a shadowy one

Smudges of charcoal immersed

with thunderclouds and steam filled glasses

My toes are fully submerged in the land beneath me

INDIGENOUS, I AM

I have two feet grounded in the present

I feel my body get heavy with quietness

I gaze into my future and watch,

as the ball of fire so clearly peaks over the horizon

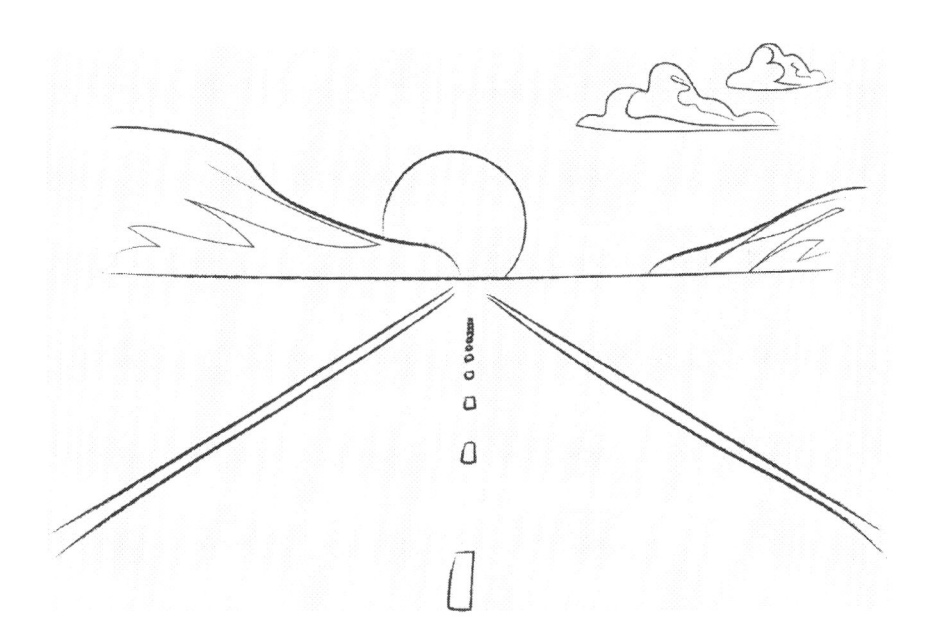

Ballads of My Path

How will I know I am on the right path?
Rather, how will I know if I am on a path where
my flowers will be cared for, where my healing will be a priority,
and my ancestors will walk beside me.

I will look in the eyes of my children,
and through their eyes I will see who they see.
I will search in the arms of my partner,
in her gentle embraces or loving nudges towards growth.

I will find it in the songs of my family.
Their melodies will always guide me to where I need to be.
I will look no further than the voice I've found within me.
My whispered hums are now thunderous ballads,

that I could never dream of burying again.

-I will walk in beauty

INDIGENOUS, I AM

INDIGENOUS, I AM

About The Author

Niłtooli is part of the Diné Nation of Arizona and the Lumbee Nation of North Carolina. She resides in the twin cities of Minnesota with her partner and family.

When she's not coaching tennis or writing, she loves to spend time with her family, spoil her two nephews, and be with her friends.

Niłtooli remembers writing poetry at a young age in her countless journals. Writing was a sense of safety when she often felt unable to speak and felt unsafe. Turning to her empty pages was her early form of therapy, and her way of necessary release of the emotions she held captive.

This is her first (of many, hopefully) poetry collection.

INDIGENOUS, I AM

More From Eaglespeaker Publishing

UNeducation: A Residential School Graphic Novel

Napi The Trixster: A Blackfoot Graphic Novel

UNeducation 2: The Side of Society You Don't See on TV

Napi Children's Books

COLLABORATIONS:

Young Water Protectors

The Empowerment of Eahwahewi

Hello … Fruit Basket

How The Earth Was Created

I Am The Opioid Crisis

My Ribbon Skirts

The Secret of the Stars

Aahksoyo'p Nootski Cookbook

… and many many more at eaglespeaker.com

INDIGENOUS, I AM

If you absolutely loved this book, please tell your friends, then find it on AMAZON.COM and leave a quick review, even if it's just "I liked it". Your words help more than you may realize. Thanks so much.

For bulk orders, and more Indigenous awesomeness, visit
eaglespeaker.com

INDIGENOUS, I AM

Made in the USA
Columbia, SC
07 October 2021